JOSIE SMITH

at the Seashore

Also by Magdalen Nabb
JOSIE SMITH

JOSIE SMITH
at the Seashore

Magdalen Nabb

illustrated by Pirkko Vainio

Margaret K. McElderry Books
NEW YORK

Certain words in this story have been changed for American readers
with the author's approval.

Margaret K. McElderry Books
Macmillan Publishing Company
866 Third Avenue
New York, NY 10022

Text copyright © 1989 by Magdalen Nabb
Illustrations copyright © 1989 by Pirkko Vainio
First published 1989 by William Collins Sons & Co. Ltd.

Printed in the United States of America
10 9 8 7 6 5 4 3 2 1

Library of Congress Cataloging-in-Publication Data
Nabb, Magdalen.
Josie Smith at the seashore / Magdalen Nabb. — 1st U.S. ed.
p. cm.
Summary: Six-year-old Josie's day at the beach with Mom and Gran
is highlighted by a donkey ride, making a dog friend, and getting lost.
[1. Seashore—Fiction.] I. Vainio, Pirkko, ill. II. Title.
PZ7.N125Jos 1990   [E]—dc20   89-8168   CIP   AC
ISBN 0-689-50492-6

Contents

A Present
for Eileen

A Present
for Eileen

Josie Smith was sitting at the table but she
wasn't eating anything.

"Eat your breakfast," said Josie's mom.

"I'm not hungry," said Josie Smith.
"Are we going yet?"

"Not until your gran comes," said
Josie's mom, "and not until you've eaten
your breakfast."

Josie Smith tried to eat her breakfast,
but the things on her plate grew bigger and
bigger instead of getting smaller.

When she looked out of the kitchen
window she saw a sunbeam making a glittery square on the wall in the yard. The

sunbeam had specks of dust twirling round and round in it and Josie Smith's tummy felt all wobbly when she looked at it because she was going to the seashore.

"Are we staying all day?" asked Josie Smith.

"Yes," said Josie's mom.

"But how will we have our lunch?"

"We'll have sandwiches on the beach," said Josie's mom.

"My tummy's all wobbly," said Josie Smith.

"That's because you're too excited," said Josie's mom.

"Can I get down and go and see if my gran's coming?"

"Put your sweater on," said Josie's mom, "and fasten your shoes or you'll fall."

Josie Smith put her sweater on and fastened the buckles on her best white sandals. She wasn't wearing her rubber boots because she was going to the seashore. She got her bucket and spade and went *slap slap slap* in her best white sandals to the front door and opened it.

Josie's house was number 1. It was the

same as all the other houses in the street and
the street was the same as all the other streets
on the side of the hill, and on top of the hill
there was a tower. At the bottom of the hill
were Josie Smith's school and the main road
and shops and the mills with tall chimneys.

Josie Smith stood on the doorstep and
smelled the sunshine. Mrs. Chadwick came
out of her corner shop across the road and
started sweeping her doorstep.

"My word," said Mrs. Chadwick. "You
look posh."

"I am posh," said Josie Smith. "I'm going to the seashore when my gran comes."

"No!" said Mrs. Chadwick. "I don't believe you. You're kidding me!"

Josie Smith pointed her toe in her best white sandals so that Mrs. Chadwick would notice them, and she held her bucket and spade as tight as she could so that Mrs. Chadwick would notice those, too.

"I won't be coming for any candy today," she told Mrs. Chadwick, "because I have to save my spending money for the seashore."

"Is that right?" said Mrs. Chadwick. "And what are you going to buy with it when you get there?"

"A bottle of pop with a straw," said Josie Smith, "and an ice-cream cone and some flags for my sand castles."

"Well, I hope you enjoy yourself," said Mrs. Chadwick, "and don't sit down on the doorstep in that posh dress." She went back in her shop and shut the door, making the bell ring.

Josie Smith waited on the doorstep, smelling the sunshine.

Eileen came out of the house next door, pushing her squeaky doll's carriage.

"Are you playing?" Eileen said.

"No," said Josie Smith, and she put her bucket and spade down on the step and started whizzing round and round as fast as she could on the pavement to make her skirt twirl up.

"You're showing your pants," Eileen said.

"I don't care," said Josie Smith. Then she stood still.

"What have you got your best dress on for?" Eileen asked.

"I'm going to the seashore," said Josie Smith.

"So am I," Eileen said, "next week, and we're staying for two weeks in a boarding-house."

"What's a boardinghouse?" asked Josie Smith. "Is it made of boards?"

"No..." said Eileen, and then she said, "It's a bit made of boards but not all of it."

"I don't want to go in a boarding-house," Josie Smith said. "We're going to have our lunch on the beach and I'm going to have a bottle of pop with a straw and an ice-cream cone and some flags for my sand castles." And she started whizzing round again to make her skirt twirl up.

"Show-off," Eileen said.

"Just because you can't come!" shouted Josie Smith, whizzing round.

"I don't care," said Eileen, "and anyway, my best dress is pink."

Josie Smith stopped whizzing around. She looked down at her best dress. It was white organdy with little red and blue velvet spots on it and a blue velvet ribbon round the waist.

"Mine's better than yours," said Josie Smith. "My mom made it specially."

"Mine's from a shop," said Eileen, "and it's pink."

"I don't care," said Josie Smith, "and anyway, pink's soppy."

"Yours is scruffy," Eileen said, "and spotty."

"You're spotty!" shouted Josie Smith. "You've got freckles and you're spotty all over!"

Eileen pinched Josie Smith hard on the

arm. Then she stamped off down the street with her squeaky doll's carriage. When she got to the bottom she squeaked all the way up again and in at her own front door. When she came back out she was wearing her mom's high-heeled shoes.

"Show-off," said Josie Smith, and went in.

Josie's mom was putting her white jacket on. There was a big basket on the chair with towels and a thermos in it.

"Mom," said Josie Smith, "when I grow out of this dress can I have a pink one?"

"I've only just made you that," said Josie's mom, "and I can let it down next summer."

"But when I *do* grow out of it, can I?"

"We'll see," said Josie's mom.

"Why do you always say 'We'll see'?" asked Josie Smith.

"Because we'll have to see," said Josie's mom. "Now button your sweater properly, your gran's at the door."

"You do look a treat," said Josie's gran when she came in. "Are you ready to go?"

"Yes," said Josie Smith.

When they set off, Eileen was sitting on her doorstep, still wearing her mom's high heels. She looked as if she'd been crying. Josie Smith looked at her when they walked past to make sure Eileen saw her going to the seashore, and she saw her rubbing her eyes and sniffing. Josie Smith walked down the street with her gran on one side and her mom on the other side, pointing her toes in her best white sandals. But halfway down the street she stopped.

"What's the matter?" asked Josie's mom.

"Why have you stopped?" asked Josie's gran.

Josie Smith turned round. At the top of the street Eileen was still sitting in the corner of her doorstep by herself, watching them. A big lump came into Josie Smith's throat.

"Can Eileen come?" she said in a very small voice.

"No," said Josie's mom. "We can't afford to take Eileen."

"But she's my best friend," said Josie

11

Smith, "and she's all by herself."

"Don't you worry about Eileen," said Josie's mom. "She'll be going away for two weeks."

"But not today," said Josie Smith. "She's by herself with nobody to play with. I want to stay at home with Eileen!" And Josie Smith began to roar.

"We're going to miss the train," said Josie's mom. "Behave yourself!" She started pulling Josie Smith's hand, but Josie Smith only roared louder and louder. She roared so loud that she couldn't hear what her mom was shouting. Josie's mom pulled and Josie's gran pulled, but Josie Smith wouldn't go.

"I don't want to go to the seashore anymore!" roared Josie Smith. "I don't want to!"

"She's too excited," said Josie's mom. "I knew this would happen."

Then Josie's gran bent down and put her arm around Josie Smith and whispered in her ear.

"Listen to me. Are you listening?"

"No-o-o!" roared Josie Smith.

"You've got some spending money, haven't you?" asked Josie's gran.

"Ye-es!" roared Josie Smith.

"Well, listen. When we get to the seashore you'll see all sorts of nice things to buy and you can bring a nice present back for Eileen."

Josie Smith stopped roaring and sniffed.

"Would you like that?" asked Josie's gran.

"Yes," said Josie Smith.

"All right then," said Josie's gran, getting a handkerchief out of her handbag. "Stand still while I dry your eyes."

Josie Smith stood still.

"Blow," said Josie's gran.

Josie Smith blew.

"Right," said Josie's gran, putting the handkerchief away. "Now what in the world's this that I've found in my handbag?"

"Is it your magic handbag?" asked Josie Smith.

"It must be," said Josie's gran, "because

there's a bag of caramels in here and *I* don't know how it got there. Shall we all have one?"

"Yes," said Josie Smith, and they set off again.

When they got on the train, Josie Smith said, "Will I be sick?"

"No," said Josie's mom, "not if you sit still."

So Josie Smith sat still with her best dress spread out round her as far as it would go and was good all the way. When they got off the train there were big shops and cars and buses and crowds of people.

"Where's the sea?" asked Josie Smith.

"At the end of this street," said Josie's gran. "Can't you smell it?"

Josie Smith held on tight as they walked and closed her eyes and sniffed. There was a candy-floss smell and a fish-and-chip smell and a bathing-suit smell and a windy salty smell.

"Look," said Josie's mom, and lifted her up.

Josie Smith opened her eyes and saw a wide blue sky that was much higher than the

one at home, and far away, where the sky ended, was a glittery silvery stripe of sea. Then Josie Smith looked down over the railings and saw the sand with deck chairs all along.

"How will we get down to the sand?" asked Josie Smith.

"There are steps," said Josie's mom, and they walked along the sandy pavement with the wind blowing their breath away until they were almost at the steps. Then Josie Smith stopped.

"Come on," said Josie's mom.

"Look!" shouted Josie Smith, jumping up and down as hard as she could so that they would listen. "Look! Over there!" There was a big booth with a blue-and-white-striped roof and it was covered all over with shining pink and blue balloons bouncing on long strings and tubs full of new spades and beach balls and spotted balls and striped balls and streamers and whistles and red, white, and blue flags flapping and shiny plastic windmills going *whrrr-ap-ap-ap* in the wind.

"Eileen's present!" shouted Josie Smith.

"We can come back later," said Josie's mom.

But Josie Smith didn't want to come back later. There were hundreds of people walking up and down and if they bought all the things from the booth there would be nothing left for Eileen.

"Well, don't spend all your money," said Josie's mom.

Josie Smith ran to the booth and stood on her toes. At the back inside it there were a lot of brown woolly monkeys with wrinkly faces hanging on strings, and in the middle was a wrinkly lady's face with red lips and brown woolly hair.

"I want a present for Eileen," said Josie Smith, and then she remembered and said, "please."

The wrinkly lady's face didn't smile. Perhaps she wanted to keep all the toys for herself. Josie Smith looked at her and then she looked at everything. She liked the windmills best. They were in a big bucket.

Red-and-white ones, blue-and-white ones,
and a giant pink one in the middle.

"Can I have a windmill?" asked Josie
Smith.

The wrinkly lady's face didn't say
anything, but a hand with a lot of rings on it,
and red fingernails, reached over and started
to pull out a blue-and-white windmill.

"Not that one," said Josie Smith.
"Eileen likes pink."

"That's a dollar."

Josie Smith took the giant pink wind-mill and put all of her spending money into the hand with the rings and the red fingernails.

"Good gracious!" said Josie's gran when Josie Smith came running back. "Whatever have you gone and bought?"

"It's a windmill," said Josie Smith, "for Eileen."

"If you've spent all your money on that," said Josie's mom, "I don't want to hear you saying 'Can I have, can I have?' all day long."

"I won't," said Josie Smith, and they went down the sandy steps and got two deck chairs for Josie's mom and Josie's gran to sit in. Josie Smith planted Eileen's windmill in the sand in between them.

All the children on the beach were digging. Josie Smith started digging, too. She dug a big hole and sat in it and then she made the sand she'd dug out into a big castle and patted it. Then she ran round and round the castle until she couldn't run anymore. She had sand in her toes and sand in her ears and sand all over her dress, and she felt very, very thirsty.

"I'm thirsty," said Josie Smith, and she was just going to say "Can I have a bottle of pop?" when she remembered. She'd spent all her money on Eileen's windmill.

"What's the matter?" said Josie's gran. "Are you wishing you still had your spending money?"

"No," said Josie Smith. But she said it with her eyes shut because it was a lie.

"If you're thirsty," said Josie's mom, "you can drink some tea from the thermos."

Josie Smith drank the tea, but she didn't like it. And Eileen's big pink windmill went *whrrr-ap-ap-ap*, flapping and shining in the wind.

Josie Smith went back to her digging. She filled her bucket ten times and made ten little sand castles all round the big one. Then she dug a long, long path from her castles toward the sea and ran up and down it until she couldn't run anymore. She had sand in her fingers and sand in her hair and sand all over her legs, and she felt very, very hungry.

"I'm hungry," said Josie Smith, and she

was just going to say "Can I have an ice-cream cone?" when she remembered. She'd spent all her money on Eileen's windmill.

"What's the matter?" said Josie's gran. "Are you wishing you still had your spending money?"

"No," said Josie Smith, but she said it with her eyes shut because it was a lie.

"If you're hungry," said Josie's mom, "you can have an apple from the basket."

Josie Smith ate the apple, but she didn't like it. And Eileen's big pink windmill went *whrrr-ap-ap-ap*, flapping and shining in the wind.

Josie Smith went back to her castles. She collected shells and filled her bucket with them and took them to her path and made it fancy with them. Then she stood back and looked. She had sand on her elbows and sand on her knees and sand on the end of her nose. The castles were finished.

"It's finished," said Josie Smith, and she was just going to say "Can I have some flags for it?" when she remembered. She'd spent all her money on Eileen's windmill.

"What's the matter?" said Josie's gran. "Are you wishing you still had your spending money?"

Josie Smith closed her eyes and tried to say "No," but she couldn't. She closed her eyes tighter and some little tears squeezed out. She opened her eyes and looked up the beach and down the beach and saw everybody else's castles with red, white, and blue flags on them.

"I don't want to dig anymore," said Josie Smith, and her face felt hot and tired.

"If you're tired," said Josie's gran, "you can sit in my deck chair. I'm going for a little walk. And if you're careful with them you can wear my sunglasses as well. Do you want to?"

"Yes," said Josie Smith. And she sat in her gran's deck chair and looked through her gran's sunglasses that made the sea look brown and sad. All the other children were shouting and laughing because they all had flags for their sand castles. Josie Smith didn't like the seashore so much anymore. She wanted to go home.

"Here I am," said Josie's gran. "Up you
get from my deck chair."

Josie Smith got up.

"Ah," said Josie's gran, sitting down.
"I'm really enjoying myself. I just wish I had
a big sand castle like yours, but I'm too old to
build one."

"You can have mine," said Josie Smith.
"I don't like it anymore."

"Well," said Josie's gran, "that's very

nice of you, but I like a sand castle with flags on it, myself."

"I haven't got any flags," said Josie Smith, and some more tears squeezed out and rolled down under her gran's sunglasses.

"You haven't got any flags?" said Josie's gran. "Well, a sand castle's no good without flags. We'd better see if there are any in that magic handbag of mine. Did you forget I'd brought my magic handbag?"

"Yes," said Josie Smith. "Will there really be flags in it?"

And she stared hard at the handbag.

"Well," said Josie's gran, "you never know with magic handbags what there'll be. But we need some flags for our castle, don't we?"

"Yes," said Josie Smith.

"And you've been good. You bought a nice present for Eileen and you haven't said 'Can I have?' even once, have you?"

"No," said Josie Smith.

"In that case," said Josie's gran, "it's bound to be all right."

And she opened the magic handbag and

out came a bundle of brand-new red, white, and blue flags. "There we are," said Josie's gran. "You go and put them on for us."

"Mom!" shouted Josie Smith when the flags were flying on the castle. "Mom! Look!"

"Well!" said Josie's mom. "I think that's the best sand castle I've ever seen. Come and sit on my knee and have a rest where we can look at it."

So Josie Smith sat on her mom's knee in the deck chair and looked and tried to decide what was the best thing in all the world: the sand castle with its red, white, and blue flags flapping or the glittering silver sea or her gran's magic handbag or Eileen's big pink windmill going *whrrr-ap-ap-ap*, flapping and shining in the wind.

Josie Smith's
New Friend

Josie Smith's
New Friend

Josie Smith was sitting on the beach eating sandwiches. Her mom and her gran were sitting in their deck chairs eating sandwiches, too. The sun was shining and the wind was blowing. Josie Smith ate a sandwich with sardines in it and a sandwich with cheese in it and a sandwich with tomatoes in it. All of the sandwiches had sand in them, too.

"There's sand in it," said Josie Smith when she started eating another one. "Is that why they're called sandwiches, because there's sand in them?"

"There's sand in them," said Josie's mom, "because you keep getting sand all over your fingers." And she cleaned Josie Smith's hands again with the sponge from the big basket. "Now be more careful."

"I am being careful," said Josie Smith.

"She's doing her best," said Josie's gran, "but this wind's blowing sand everywhere."

"Can I have some cake now?" asked Josie Smith. She ate some cake and then some more cake and then they all had a drink of tea from the thermos in the big basket.

When everything was put away, Josie's mom said, "Now, we want five minutes' peace and quiet." She got out her newspaper and Josie's gran got out her knitting.

Josie Smith sat on the sand and looked up at the pages of her mom's newspaper. She could read a lot of the words, but she couldn't understand the stories and she didn't like the pictures because they weren't colored. So then she looked at her gran's knitting. Her gran had put her glasses on, but she never looked down at her knitting. She looked at the sea and she looked at the people in the other deck chairs and the children digging in the sand, but her fingers

did the knitting by themselves. She was knitting a sweater for Josie Smith.

"When will it be ready?" asked Josie Smith.

"Not today," said Josie's gran.

"But when will it?" asked Josie Smith.

"Don't pester," said Josie's mom behind her newspaper. "I told you we want five minutes' peace and quiet."

Josie Smith didn't like peace and quiet.

Only grown-ups like peace and quiet and they never get fed up with it, but Josie Smith got fed up. She looked at her gran's watch to see if five minutes had gone past, but they hadn't.

"When can I go in the sea?" asked Josie Smith.

"Not yet," said Josie's mom.

"But when can I?" asked Josie Smith.

"We'll see," said Josie's mom, "and don't let me have to tell you again: Don't pester."

Josie Smith stopped pestering. She sat in the sand and dug with her heels to make holes for her feet to fit in. Then she collected sand from all around her and poured it over her feet so that they disappeared under little sand hills. But right in front of the little sand hills she saw two more feet. Somebody else's feet in red plastic sandals. Josie Smith looked up. There was a girl watching her. A girl with black pigtails and a red-and-white-striped dress.

"What's your name?" said the girl with the black pigtails.

"Josie Smith," said Josie Smith.

"Mine's Rosie Margaret," said the girl
with the black pigtails, "and it's my birthday
today and I'm six."

"So am I," said Josie Smith, shutting
her eyes when she said it because really she
was only five and three-quarters.

"And now that I'm six," said Rosie
Margaret, "I'm going to have piano lessons."

"So am I," said Josie Smith, and she

didn't know if she should shut her eyes or not when she said it. She didn't know what piano lessons meant, so she wasn't sure whether she'd be having them or not.

"You can be my friend, if you want," Rosie Margaret said.

Josie Smith stared up at Rosie Margaret, but she didn't say anything. Rosie Margaret had thin legs and fingers and frightening green eyes.

"I've got a beach ball," Rosie Margaret said, "and I'll let you play with it and I've got a whole bag of candy."

Josie Smith filled her bucket with sand but she didn't say anything.

"I've got loads of spending money as well," said Rosie Margaret.

Josie Smith went on filling her bucket, but she saw Rosie Margaret's thin fingers go in the pocket of her red-and-white-striped dress and pull out a shiny, red purse with red glitter on it. The purse was fat with pennies.

"We can have a ride on the donkeys," said Rosie Margaret, "when they come."

Josie Smith stopped filling her bucket.

"What donkeys?" she said.

"The donkeys that come on the beach," said Rosie Margaret, pointing, "down there. Have you never been on them?"

"No," said Josie Smith.

"I have, loads of times," said Rosie Margaret, "every day."

"Are they real donkeys?" asked Josie Smith.

"Of course they are," said Rosie Margaret. "Anybody knows that. I can pay for a ride for us both, only you have to be my friend first."

"All right," said Josie Smith, and she forgot about Rosie Margaret's frightening green eyes because she was excited about the donkeys. "We can play going up the wall while we're waiting."

So they went round the back of the deck chairs and tucked their dresses in their pants and tipped upside down on their hands with their feet against the high pebbly wall.

When they were upside down, Rosie Margaret said, "Is that big pink windmill yours?"

"Yes," said Josie Smith.

"You have to let me play with it as well, then, now you're my friend."

"We can't play with it," Josie Smith said. "It's not for me. It's a present for Eileen."

"Who's Eileen?" Rosie Margaret said.

"My best friend," said Josie Smith.

"My best friend's called Jennifer," Rosie Margaret said. "She's staying in the same boardinghouse as me and she's gone shopping with her mom and she's getting a new dress."

"I've got my best dress on," said Josie Smith.

They stayed upside down for a long time, looking at the upside-down deck chairs and the upside-down sea.

When they stood up and untucked their dresses, Rosie Margaret said, "I like your best dress. I'm going to get one the same."

"My mom made it," said Josie Smith. Then she said, "Shall we play with your beach ball now?"

"No," said Rosie Margaret. "I don't want to."

"You promised," said Josie Smith.

"I never," said Rosie Margaret, "I only said. I never promised."

They sat down on the sand behind the deck chairs near Eileen's windmill that was flapping and shining in the wind. Josie Smith waited to see if Rosie Margaret would give her a piece of candy, but she didn't.

Rosie Margaret put her arm round Josie Smith and whispered in her ear, "I know what, we'll get my mom's lipstick out of her handbag and put some on."

Josie Smith was scared. "You'll get

smacked," she said, "for going in your mom's handbag without asking."

"My mom never smacks me," said Rosie Margaret. "She lets me do anything I want. Only my dad smacks because he's bad tempered. Does your dad smack?"

"No," said Josie Smith. "He lets me do anything I want." But she shut her eyes tight when she said it because she didn't have a dad.

"Come on," said Rosie Margaret, and she crawled along the sand until she was behind her mom's deck chair. Josie Smith crawled along behind her and then she sat down and watched. Rosie Margaret got her mom's handbag out from under the deck chair and opened it.

Josie Smith's chest went *bam-bam-bam* because she was scared, but Rosie Margaret wasn't scared. She tipped everything out of the handbag until she found the lipstick and then she pushed all the other things back in with sand mixed up in them. Josie Smith wanted to run away, but she liked looking at the lipstick. Rosie Margaret screwed it

round and round and made the red bit come
up as far as it would go.

"Look," she said, and she pushed out
her lips and chin and put some lipstick on
just like a real grown-up lady.

"Can I try as well?" whispered Josie
Smith.

"If you want," said Rosie Margaret, and
she gave the lipstick to Josie Smith.

Josie Smith pushed out her chin and her
lips like she'd seen her mom do and started to
push the lipstick against them. Some of it got
on her nose and some of it got on her chin

and then she felt it getting on her teeth, so she shut her lips tight and crayoned it hard against them. Snap! The lipstick broke. The red piece broke right off and fell in the sand.

Josie Smith jumped up and Rosie Margaret jumped up and they both ran away as fast as they could. When they stopped, Josie Smith's chest was going *bam-bam-bam* as fast as lightning because she was scared. Rosie Margaret wasn't scared. She whizzed round and round on the sand with her arms and pigtails out and she shouted, "Let's go in the sea!"

"I can't," said Josie Smith. "My mom says I can't go in by myself."

"I can go in by myself when I want," Rosie Margaret said, "because I can swim."

"I can swim as well," said Josie Smith, shutting her eyes tight because it was a lie. She waited to see if Rosie Margaret would go in the sea by herself, but she didn't. Perhaps she didn't want to. She came up close to Josie Smith and whispered in her ear, "I won't tell anybody you broke my mom's lipstick because you're my friend." Then she said,

"Let's go back and get my bag of candy."

"We can't," said Josie Smith. "Your mom'll catch us and see our lipstick."

"I don't care," Rosie Margaret said. "I'm going. You wait here if you want."

Josie Smith stood there on the sand and waited, but Rosie Margaret didn't come back. She waited a long, long time and Rosie Margaret still didn't come back.

Then she saw the donkeys. They were coming along the sand all together. There were brown donkeys and black donkeys, big donkeys and small donkeys. They had long pointy ears and ribbons in their hair and bells that jingled as they walked, and there was a man at the side with a stick, saying, "Gee up! Gee up! Ho!"

Then they all stopped with their bells still jingling.

And then Rosie Margaret came back. She didn't bring the bag of candy with her, she brought another girl. They came up and stared at Josie Smith and Rosie Margaret said, "I'm playing with Jennifer now because she's my best friend."

"Can I play as well?" asked Josie Smith.

Rosie Margaret put her arm round Jennifer and whispered to her for a long time. Then Jennifer whispered to Rosie Margaret and they started giggling.

Rosie Margaret said to Josie Smith, "You can play with us, if you want. We're playing hide and seek and you're it. You have to go behind the deck chairs and shut your eyes and count to ten."

Josie Smith went behind the deck chairs where Eileen's windmill stood flapping and shining in the wind. She shut her eyes and covered them with her hands.

"One-two-three-four-five," counted Josie Smith. She could hear Rosie Margaret whispering and she could hear Jennifer giggling.

"Six-seven-eight-nine-ten," counted Josie Smith. Then she opened her eyes. Rosie Margaret was gone and Jennifer was gone. There was nothing in between the two deck chairs except a little hole in the sand. Josie Smith began to run. Her chest hurt and she was nearly crying. She saw Rosie Margaret and Jennifer running toward the donkeys, and Rosie Margaret had Eileen's windmill in her hand. When Josie Smith caught up with them the big pink windmill was lying on the sand and the donkey man was lifting Rosie Margaret onto a brown donkey. Then he lifted Jennifer onto another one. Josie Smith picked up the windmill and stood watching. The donkey man was lifting more children up. Rosie Margaret had promised Josie Smith a ride, but the donkeys would soon be all full. Rosie Margaret and Jennifer looked down at Josie Smith from high up on the donkeys and Jennifer said, "Cry-baby, cry-baby, with your stupid windmill."

Josie Smith held Eileen's windmill tighter and Rosie Margaret looked down at her with frightening green eyes and said, "Cry-baby, cry-baby in your horrible spotty dress. You broke my mom's lipstick and left it in the sand and I'm going to tell on you."

The donkey man said, "Gee up! Gee up! Ho!" And the donkeys set off.

Josie Smith stood holding Eileen's windmill and watched them go away along

the beach with their bells jingling. They
went a long way and then the man shouted
and made them all turn round and start
walking back with their bells jingling.
When they came to where Josie Smith was
standing the man turned them round again
and then said, "Whoa!" The donkeys
stopped. When Rosie Margaret and Jennifer
were lifted down they ran off together,
laughing, without looking at Josie Smith.

Josie Smith ran after them, but she
couldn't catch up with them, so she turned
round and ran back because she wanted to
look at the donkeys. She liked all the
donkeys, but the best one was a big browny-
black one with black hair and red and white
ribbons. Its ears were bigger than all the
other donkeys' ears and it looked at Josie
Smith with a friendly face. All the donkeys
had their names on the strap across their

noses and the best big browny-black one was called Susie.

Josie Smith watched a lot more children being lifted on by the donkey man. He lifted a boy onto Susie. He was bigger than Josie Smith, but when the man let go he started crying.

"I want to get down!" screamed the boy. "Get me down!"

"Here," said the donkey man, "we'll put you on little Gypsy, then. She's the smallest."

"Get me down!" screamed the boy when the man put him on little Gypsy. "I don't want to! Get me down!" So the donkey man lifted him off and the boy ran away crying, as fast as he could go.

Josie Smith stood watching. The donkey man looked at Josie Smith and winked. "Bit of a softie," he said. "What do you say?"

"Yes," said Josie Smith.

Most of the donkeys were full. The man looked around, but no more children came. Then he said, "Paid for a ride, he did, and then ran off without asking for his money back. Come on, let's be having you. You might as well have the ride he paid for, since there's nobody else coming."

Josie Smith went to be lifted up. "My windmill," she said.

"Give it to me," the donkey man said. "I'll carry it with my stick." He lifted Josie Smith up. "You're only the size of a rabbit," he said. "We'll put you on little Gypsy."

But Josie Smith didn't want to go on little Gypsy. "I like Susie," she said, looking hard at the donkey man's brown face.

"Susie it is, then," said the donkey man, and he put her up on Susie's back. It was so high up that Josie Smith felt her head wobbling in the sky and she couldn't find the place to put her feet like the other children were doing.

"I can't reach the pedals," said Josie Smith.

"Not pedals, stirrups," said the donkey man, and he pushed Josie Smith's leg forward and pulled at some straps. "That's as short as it'll go," he said. "Now the other

one. There. She's too big for you is Susie. Are you sure you're not frightened?"

"No," said Josie Smith.

"She's a trotter is our Susie. Keep a tight hold because if the others crowd her she'll break into a trot. You keep your eye on her ears because if she flattens them you'll see she'll break into a trot. All right."

"Yes," said Josie Smith. She didn't know what the donkey man meant, but she held on tight and looked at Susie's big ears.

"Gee up! Gee up! Ho!"

The donkeys set off.

Josie Smith felt the sand on her legs rubbing against the straps and the shiny metal stirrups dangling against her feet because she still couldn't reach them properly and her head felt right up in the sky. She didn't look at the sea and she didn't look at the children on the other donkeys all around her. She only listened to the bells jingling and looked at Susie's big ears like the man had told her to do. Sometimes the big furry ears stood up straight and stiff and sometimes they turned this way and that, as if they were looking around.

"Whoa!" shouted the donkey man, and all the donkeys started to turn round and go back as if they knew the way by themselves.

Josie Smith held on tight. Little Gypsy squashed against her leg on one side and a bigger, light brown donkey squashed against her leg on the other side.

"Don't push," said Josie Smith. Then Susie's ears went down flat. "Oh!" shouted Josie Smith, and everything began to bump about. Up and down, up and down bumped Josie Smith, and the sand scratched her legs and the heavy stirrups banged and banged against her feet. Susie was right out in front of all the other donkeys and Josie Smith was holding on as tight as she could but she was slipping this way and slipping that way.

"Oh!" shouted Josie Smith.

"Whoa!" roared the donkey man, and the bumping stopped.

"You all right?" said the donkey man, getting hold of Susie's reins and stopping her.

"Yes," whispered Josie Smith, but her legs and her tummy were still wobbly after the bumping.

"Want to get off?" asked the donkey man.

"No," said Josie Smith, holding tight. She was frightened, but she didn't want to get off.

"I told you she was a trotter," said the donkey man. "Did you keep your eye on her ears?"

"Yes," said Josie Smith.

"Here," said the donkey man, and he gave Josie Smith a lump of sugar. Josie Smith was going to eat it, but the donkey man said, "Lean over and hold it out to her near the side of her head. I'll hold you on." He held Josie Smith on and she leaned over and held the sugar lump near Susie's head.

"Call her," said the donkey man. "Toh, Susie! Toh!"

"Toh, Susie! Toh!" said Josie Smith, and Susie turned around and looked at her.

"Open your hand flat," said the donkey man.

Josie Smith opened her hand flat. Susie's warm mouth took the sugar off it and she turned her head away, munching.

"Does she like it?" asked Josie Smith.

"She does that," said the donkey man. "You've made a friend for life. She'll not flatten her ears again now, you'll see."

They all set off again with their bells jingling. Josie Smith watched Susie's ears all the way back, but they didn't go down flat again. When she was lifted down she said, "Good-bye, Susie," and Susie turned and looked at her with friendly brown eyes.

"Don't forget your windmill," said the donkey man.

"Thank you," said Josie Smith, and she ran back to the deck chairs. Josie's mom was asleep, still holding her newspaper, but Josie's gran was awake.

"Whatever have you got on your face?" asked Josie's gran.

"Nothing," said Josie Smith. Then she remembered Rosie Margaret and the lipstick. But Josie's gran couldn't see very well, even when she had her glasses on, and she washed the lipstick off Josie Smith's face with the sponge without guessing what it was.

Josie's mom woke up and said, "Did you find a friend to play with? I heard you chattering."

"Yes," said Josie Smith. "Have five minutes gone past yet?"

"Just about," said Josie's mom. "Come and have a rest on my knee."

Josie Smith got on her mom's knee and snuggled down.

"Was she nice, your friend?" asked Josie's mom.

"Yes," said Josie Smith. "She had black hair with red and white ribbons and friendly brown eyes and she's my friend for life."

"Is she, now?" said Josie's mom. "And what's her name?"

"Susie," said Josie Smith. "Susie's my friend."

Josie Smith
Gets Lost

Josie Smith
Gets Lost

Josie Smith was getting ready to go in the sea. Josie's mom was getting ready, too. Josie's gran tied the strings of Josie Smith's bathing suit at the back.

"I'm nearly ready, Mom," said Josie Smith. "Are you nearly ready?"

"Nearly," said Josie's mom.

"The tide's coming right in," said Josie's gran, "so you won't have too far to walk."

"Will it come right up here?" asked Josie Smith.

"Yes," said Josie's gran. "By six o'clock it'll be splashing up against that wall behind us."

"But what about the deck chairs?" asked Josie Smith, "and the donkeys? What about Susie?"

"They'll all be gone," said Josie's gran. "And we'll be gone, too."

"Come on," said Josie's mom. "Off we go."

They walked over the soft dry sand and then over the wet hard sand and a patch of shells that hurt their feet. Then tiny waves came racing up to tickle their ankles and run away again.

"It's cold," shouted Josie Smith, hopping up and down.

"We should jump in quickly and get wet all over," said Josie's mom, "then we won't feel it so much."

So they ran as fast as they could through the waves until a bigger wave than all the others came rushing up to them —*whoosh*— and wet them all over.

"I'm wet all over!" shouted Josie Smith when the wave went away. "Even my hair's wet!"

"It doesn't matter," said Josie's mom. "It'll dry in the sun afterward."

"Look at the boy with the raft!" shouted Josie Smith. "And look at the big white duck! Look, Mom! Look at that girl's water wings! Look!"

"I am looking," said Josie's mom.

"Jump me up and down!" shouted Josie Smith.

Josie's mom got hold of her tight and jumped her up and down in the waves.

"Sploosh!" shouted Josie Smith. "Sploosh!" and she closed her eyes as she bounced up and down. Even with her eyes closed she could still see the sparkles that danced on the sea.

"I want to swim!" shouted Josie Smith. "Make me swim!"

Josie's mom turned her over on her tummy and held her tight. Josie Smith kicked and waved as hard as she could.

"Am I swimming?" shouted Josie Smith.

"Nearly," said Josie's mom.

Josie Smith kicked and waved even harder.

"Am I swimming now?" shouted Josie Smith.

"Nearly," said Josie's mom. "Don't try so hard, just enjoy the water. You'll learn in time."

But Josie Smith wanted to learn now, and she went on kicking and waving as hard as she could until she had no breath left.

"I can't swim anymore!" shouted Josie Smith.

"Float, then," said Josie's mom. She turned Josie Smith over on her back and held her tight. Josie Smith put her head on the

waves and looked at the sky as she bounced slowly up and down. She watched the seagulls flying round and calling, and she heard the children in the water all around her, squealing and shouting.

"I like floating," shouted Josie Smith. "I like floating best of all."

"Look out," said Josie's mom, and she lifted Josie Smith up higher.

But she was too late. A big roaring wave was coming right at them. Blup! Josie Smith's head was under the water. She couldn't see and she couldn't hear anything except the water roaring in her ears. Then it was light again and the children were shouting and splashing, but Josie Smith couldn't shout. She couldn't breathe. Everything in her head was stinging and she coughed and choked and choked and coughed and then she heard her mom laughing at her.

"Am I drowning?" shouted Josie Smith as soon as she could breathe again.

"No," said Josie's mom, "but you're pulling a funny face. You got a bit of water up your nose, that's all. It's nice under the water, but you mustn't try and breathe. Look." And Josie's mom held her nose and disappeared under the water so that Josie Smith could only see her hair floating on top. "You try."

Josie Smith held her nose and went under the water and heard the sea roaring. Then she popped up and heard the children shouting.

"You see," said Josie's mom. "It's good fun."

"Yes," said Josie Smith, but she didn't like it so very much because the water was too salty. "Look!" she shouted. "Look over there!"

A head was bobbing toward them on the waves. A head with its nose in the air. Not a girl's head and not a boy's head and not a grown-up's head either.

"A big dog!" shouted Josie Smith. "A big dog, swimming!"

The big dog swam right past them with his nose in the air and when he got to the shallow water he jumped up and shook

himself, wetting all the children who were paddling there. Then he ran away along the edge of the sea.

"Come on," said Josie's mom. "It's time we got out, too. We don't want to get too cold."

They came out where the tiny waves tickled their ankles and ran over the wet hard sand where the shells hurt their feet and then over the soft dry sand to the deck chairs.

Josie's gran was waiting with a big towel.

"Even my hair's wet!" shouted Josie

Smith, and she shook her head like the big dog and sprinkled water on her gran's lap. Josie's gran wrapped her up in the big towel that covered even her face and head so that her hair could be rubbed dry. But underneath the towel Josie Smith went on shouting though her gran couldn't hear all the words.

"And we saw a raft—

"And a big white duck—

"And a girl with water wings—

"And swimming—

"And floating—

"And *drowning*—

"And then a big dog came!"

"You'd better get dressed," said Josie's gran. "You can't sit in a wet bathing suit in this wind."

Josie Smith got dressed.

"I'll play with my sand castle now," she said.

She liked her sand castle with its red, white, and blue flags flapping in the wind, but she didn't like the path to it anymore because the shells along the edge were broken and sandy.

"Mom," said Josie Smith, "can I go near the sea and collect some good shells in my bucket?"

"All right," said Josie's mom, "but don't be long, and don't go in the water by yourself, even to paddle, in case a wave comes and knocks you down."

"I won't go in the water," said Josie Smith.

"And stay right in front of these deck chairs. Don't wander off or you'll get lost."

"I won't wander off," said Josie Smith. She took her bucket and set off. When she'd gone a little way toward the sea she stopped and turned around to make sure she was going in a straight line and not wandering off.

"My mom's deck chair's red-and-white striped," she said to herself, "and my gran's deck chair's green-and-white striped. And there's Eileen's windmill and the big basket in between." She turned round again and kept on going straight toward the sea.

The shells on the wet sand near the water were clean and brightly colored, pink and blue and brown and white. Some of them were striped and some were shiny inside like pearls. Josie Smith started to fill her bucket. Just when her bucket was half full and she was poking a long dark shell out of the sand with her finger, she heard something come thundering toward her from the sea. Something big and noisy and wet. Something that knocked her down, bump!

It wasn't a wave, but it was as wet as a wave and as noisy as a wave and as tall as a wave. It was the big dog who went swimming by himself in the sea.

"Oh!" shouted Josie Smith. "You shouldn't knock people over!"

The big dog shook himself and showered water all over Josie Smith.

"Oh!" shouted Josie Smith. "You shouldn't wet people!"

The big dog sat down with his tongue hanging out and thumped his tail on the sand. Josie Smith sat and looked at him. When they were both sitting down he was taller than she was.

"Do you want to play with me?" she asked him.

The big dog thumped his tail.

"I thought you did," said Josie Smith, "but you're not to knock me over."

The big dog thumped his tail. He had a collar on with his name on it.

"Can I look?" said Josie Smith. She put her face near his collar and he kept his chin up so she could read what was written on it. JIMMIE it said.

"Jimmie," said Josie Smith. "You're called Jimmie."

Jimmie thumped his tail and licked Josie Smith's face all over.

"Ugh!" said Josie Smith. "You shouldn't lick people's faces, only their hands."

Jimmie jumped up and turned his back on Josie Smith. He started digging with his front paws. Faster and faster he dug until the sand flew up and hit Josie Smith in the face.

"You shouldn't throw sand," shouted

Josie Smith. "If it gets in people's eyes, it hurts!"

Jimmie stopped digging and jumped around and around in circles with his front paws pointing.

"Stand still," said Josie Smith, "and we'll play a game. But there's no pushing over, no wetting people, and no kicking sand. Right! I'll throw a stick for you."

Josie Smith looked about on the sand until she found a good clean stick and then she threw it as far as she could into the water. Jimmie went bounding after it and swam back with it in his mouth. Then he jumped round in circles on the sand, ready to set off again. Josie Smith threw the stick ten times for him and then she said, "I'm tired now, Jimmie."

But Jimmie went on jumping round on the sand, watching for her to throw the stick again. Josie Smith sat down. Jimmie sat down, too. He put his head to one side and looked at Josie Smith and then he put his head to the other side and looked at Josie Smith. Then he saw Josie Smith's bucket.

"Woof!" he said, jumping up, and he took the handle of Josie Smith's bucket in his mouth and started running toward the sea.

"My bucket!" shouted Josie Smith, jumping up and running after him. "My bucket! Bring my bucket back! Jimmie!"

But Jimmie was running out to sea with his nose in the air and the bucket handle in his mouth.

All the people in the sea pointed at him and laughed, and when they heard Josie Smith shouting they tried to catch Jimmie and get her bucket for her, but Jimmie turned round and swam away from them. Josie Smith ran along the sand to try and keep up with him. She couldn't go in the sea by herself, and anyway, Jimmie was a long way out where the water was deep.

"Jimmie!" shouted Josie Smith. "Jimmie! Come out!"

But Jimmie went swimming along until, among all the bobbing heads and floating ducks and water wings, Josie Smith couldn't see him anymore. She stopped running and sat down on the sand. Perhaps

Jimmie would come back by himself, like he came back with the stick. She waited and waited, but Jimmie didn't come.

"I'll tell my mom on him," said Josie Smith. She got up and looked back at the deck chairs. They were blue. All of them, as far as Josie Smith could see, were blue. No red-and-white deck chair, no green-and-white deck chair, no pink windmill and no basket. The deck chairs were all blue. Josie Smith's chest started thumping, *bam-bam-bam*, like Jimmie's tail thumping the sand.

Then she remembered: she'd run along the sand after Jimmie, so she'd have to run back. She ran a long way and then stopped to look at the deck chairs. They were yellow. No red-and-white-striped ones, no green-and-white-striped ones, no pink windmill and no basket. Josie Smith's chest thumped harder, *bam-bam-bam*! Josie Smith was lost. None of the other children on the beach were lost. They were digging and playing and their moms were shouting to them and drying them and giving them things to eat. Only Josie Smith was lost. Perhaps she should try running farther, but she didn't know which way.

Then she heard a jingling noise and saw the donkeys. And the donkey man was nice and he'd tell her where the striped deck chairs were. Josie Smith started running toward the donkeys, her feet thumping the sand and her chest thumping *bam-bam-bam*. When she got to the donkeys she looked for Susie. Where was Susie? If she saw Susie, everything would be all right. If Susie was there she wasn't really lost.

"Susie," whispered Josie Smith. "Susie..." The donkeys nodded and stamped their feet and looked at her, but none of them had Susie's friendly face.

They're wearing blue ribbons now, thought Josie Smith, but they had red and white ribbons before.

She went to the front where the donkey man was bending over a sack of hay.

"Excuse me, Mr. Donkey Man," said Josie Smith.

"Too late," said the donkey man. "We're off now." He straightened up and looked at Josie Smith. It wasn't her donkey man at all! It was another man with a cap on, and he didn't know Josie Smith. He turned away and started walking off with his donkeys.

"Excuse me! Mr. Donkey Man. Excuse me!" Josie Smith trotted after him.

"Too late," said the donkey man again. "We're off."

"I don't want a ride," said Josie Smith, trotting to keep up with him. "I'm looking for a donkey that was here before, called Susie, and there was a man and he didn't

have a cap and Susie had red and white ribbons!"

"Susie?" said the donkey man with a cap. "Susie? Red and white ribbons? That'll be Jack Holt's beasts, but he's not on this patch. He's farther down. No point looking for him now, he'll have gone."

"Why will he have gone?" asked Josie Smith, still trotting.

"Tide's coming in," said the donkey man with a cap, and he went off, with all his donkeys following him.

Josie Smith stood still. She looked at the

donkeys going away and then she looked at the people in the yellow deck chairs. They were standing up. They were rolling up towels and putting them in bags. The children were putting their shoes and socks on. The grown-ups were folding their deck chairs. They were starting to go away. Something tickled Josie Smith's ankle. She looked down. A little wave had crept up to her feet. It went away again but another one was coming behind it.

"Tide's coming in," the donkey man had said.

"By six o'clock it'll be splashing up against that wall behind us," Josie's gran had said.

And the deck chairs, and the donkeys...?

"They'll all be gone," Josie's gran had said, *"and we'll be gone, too."*

Another tiny wave tickled Josie Smith's feet and went away. Josie Smith looked at the sea. It was fierce and glittering, gray and cold and deep, and it was coming nearer.

"You mustn't try and breathe," Josie's mom had said. Josie Smith held her nose and

watched the sea. Could she hold her breath under the water until the tide went out again? She remembered the water roaring in her ears and stinging in her head and choking her. The frightening gray sea was coming nearer, cold and salty, glittering and deep.

More people were going away.

Josie Smith didn't want to be lost. She didn't want to drown. She opened her mouth as far as it would go and shouted, "Mom!" And then she began to roar. She roared so hard that she couldn't hear anything else and the tears rolled down her cheeks and into her mouth, as salty as the sea. She felt somebody put a hand on her head and when she looked through her tears there were people standing all around her. She could see their legs. Bare legs, legs with dresses, legs with trousers, long legs and short legs, fat legs and thin legs. Then a man bent down near Josie Smith's face and said, "What's the matter? Have you hurt yourself?"

"No-o-o!" roared Josie Smith.

"What's the matter, then?" said the man.

"I don't want to dro-own!" roared Josie Smith.

"You're not going to drown," said the man. "Come away from the water. The tide's coming in." And when he said that, Josie Smith roared even louder.

"Perhaps she's lost," a lady said, and she bent down near Josie Smith's face. "Where's your mom?" she asked.

"I don't kno-ow!" roared Josie Smith, "because Jimmie took my bucket away!"

"Who's Jimmie?" asked the lady. "Is he your brother?"

Josie Smith just roared.

"Are your mom and dad on the beach?" asked the lady. "Where are they?"

"Near Susie," roared Josie Smith. "But Susie's gone!"

"Who's Susie?" asked the lady. "Is she your sister?"

Josie Smith just roared.

"Perhaps she knows where they're staying," the man said. "That might help."

"Do you know where your house is?" asked the lady.

"Across from Mrs. Chadwick's shop," roared Josie Smith. "I want my mom!"

"We'll find your mom," the lady said. "If you'll just stop crying and tell me your name, I promise we'll find your mom. That's better. Now then, what's your name?"

"Josie Smith," said Josie Smith.

"Right, you come with me." She got hold of Josie Smith's hand and took her to the steps near the pebbly wall and up to the sandy pavement where the railings went along. Then they climbed a little step into a trailer where a boy was sitting holding a teddy bear and a nice lady was writing in a book at a desk.

"This is Josie Smith," said the lady who was holding her hand. "She got lost on the beach. She's got a brother called Jimmie and a sister called Susie."

"She'll be all right here," said the nice lady who was writing in a book. And the other lady went away.

"Sit down, Josie," said the nice lady, "and tell me what you'd like to play with."

Josie Smith looked around her. There were toys everywhere. She'd never been in a trailer before and she didn't know they were full of toys. Josie Smith looked at them all and then she chose. "The big doll," she said.

The nice lady gave the big doll to Josie Smith. It was nearly as big as she was. Josie Smith sat it on her knee and sniffed its hair. The boy who was holding the teddy bear didn't play with it. He just sat still. Josie Smith sat still, too. They were both sitting on stools. Josie Smith looked all around the

trailer, but she couldn't see any beds to sleep in or any food to eat.

"Where will I go to sleep?" Josie Smith asked the nice lady.

"Are you tired?" the lady asked.

"No," said Josie Smith.

"Do you know where you are?" asked the lady.

"No," said Josie Smith.

"This is the lost children's trailer," the lady said.

"Will I have to live here forever," asked Josie Smith, "now that I'm a lost child?"

"No," the lady said. "I'm going to make an announcement and your mom will hear it and come for you."

The nice lady pressed a switch and then said in a loud voice, "Will the parents of Josie Smith, the parents of Josie Smith, please come to the lost children's trailer? Will the parents of Josie Smith, the parents of Josie Smith, please come to the lost children's trailer?"

"Can my mom hear you?" asked Josie Smith.

"Yes," said the lady, "everybody on the beach will hear. Your mom will come now, you wait and see."

And as soon as she said it, the door of the trailer opened and Josie Smith jumped up, ready to go to her mom.

But it wasn't Josie's mom. It was a man, and he took the boy away and the boy cried because they took the teddy bear away from him before he went.

Josie Smith sat down again and waited, sniffing the big doll's hair. There was a big lump hurting her throat because nobody came for her. Perhaps her mom and her gran had gone home on the train because the tide had come in. Some tears squeezed out of her eyes but she didn't make a noise. She held the big doll tighter. Then she said in a small voice, "I feel sick."

"Don't worry," the nice lady said. "Your mom will come."

But her mom didn't come.

Josie Smith tried not to cry out loud, but it was hard to breathe because of the lump in her throat, and she felt cold all over.

"I feel cold," said Josie Smith.

Then she heard a noise at the door. A scratching noise and a thumping noise.

"That's funny," the nice lady said, "perhaps the door's stuck. Maybe this is your mom." She got up and opened the door.

Josie Smith looked, but she didn't see her mom.

She saw a bucket. Then she saw a nose and big ears. And then in came Jimmie, panting and thumping his tail.

"It's Jimmie!" shouted Josie Smith.

"Is it your dog?" asked the nice lady.

"No," said Josie Smith. "But it's my bucket!"

And then in came Josie's mom and Josie's gran.

"Thank goodness we've found you!" said Josie's mom.

"This dog brought us all the way here," said Josie's gran.

And then they said "Thank you" to the nice lady and took Josie Smith away.

When they were on the train going home, Josie Smith snuggled down on the seat between her mom and her gran and said, "Tell me again about Jimmie finding me."

"I've told you three times already," said Josie's mom.

"Tell me again," said Josie Smith.

"Well," said Josie's mom, "first of all we looked up and there was no Josie. Then we walked up and down the beach."

"And no Josie," said Josie Smith.

"And no Josie," said Josie's mom. "And then along came Jimmie and he had a bucket in his mouth that looked like yours."

"It *was* mine!" said Josie Smith.

"It was yours," said Josie's mom, "and

it still had a few shells in it. And Jimmie
jumped around and around in the sand and
kept running off and running back, trying to
make us follow him, so follow him we did.
He took us everywhere you'd been, and the
people who'd seen you told us you'd been
taken to the lost children's trailer, and we
thought, where's that?"

"But Jimmie knew," said Josie Smith.

"Jimmie knew," said Josie's mom, "but
he ran so fast it was hard to follow him

because we were carrying the big basket and Eileen's windmill. But he kept coming back to make sure we were still there. We were already on our way to the trailer when we heard them announce your name."

"But where's Jimmie now?" asked Josie Smith.

"We don't know," said Josie's mom. "Once he'd found you and given you your bucket back, he ran off."

"But he won't stay out in the dark by himself with no dinner, will he?" asked Josie Smith.

"No," said Josie's mom, "he'll have gone home. Dogs don't get lost."

"And donkeys?" asked Josie Smith.

"Donkeys don't get lost either," said Josie's mom. "Susie will be at home having some dinner, too."

"And then what happened?" said Josie Smith. "Tell me."

"And then Jimmie jumped into the trailer," said Josie's mom, "and we went in, too, and we saw you with the big doll on your knee. And then..."

But when Josie's mom looked down she

saw that Josie Smith's eyes were closed.

Josie Smith was fast asleep. And all the time the train was taking her home she dreamed a long dream all about Jimmie running with the bucket in his mouth beside the glittering silver sea, and the sand rubbing her legs as Susie trotted with her big ears down, and Rosie Margaret and the lipstick, and Eileen's big pink windmill turning and flapping and shining in the wind.

$$3188$$
$$3112$$
$$\overline{6300}$$